THE EXPERIENCE

OF

GROWTH

THE EXPERIENCE

OF

GROWTH

ROBERT BAYARD

www.astapublications.com

Library of Congress Cataloging-in-Publication Data

Bayard, A., Robert, The Experience of Growth
p. cm
Includes index.

ISBN13: 978-1-934947-29-6
LCCN:

1. Young Adult Fiction 2. Urban Fiction. 3. Drama Fiction.
I. Title

Printed in the United States of America

Acknowledgments

Many thanks to GOD, for his immeasurable love, guidance and countless blessings; My family members and friends, who have remained supportive throughout my trials and tribulations; My wife, who has been a great friend and wonderful mother to our children; Mom for showing me the true meaning of strength and patience.

I would like to thank every reader of this book, for allowing my thoughts to influence some form of positive change.

THE EXPERIENCE

OF

GROWTH

ABOUT THE AUTHOR

Robert Bayard was born and raised in Camden, NJ and graduated from college in 2001. He worked as a Mental Health counselor for five years, servicing juvenile and adult populations. He still resides in New Jersey, working within the social services field.

THE EXPERIENCE

OF

GROWTH

ROBERT BAYARD

ASTA
PUBLICATIONS ™

CHAPTER

1

Underneath dim street lights that battled darkness, I lit a cigarette after selling my last bag of crack. At that time, my learned behaviors resembled millions of teenage youth living in urban areas throughout the United States.

Regretfully, this self-destructing and murderous conduct has become acceptable by certain social groups, but ultimately it was profitable to my employer and remains profitable to the employers of today's criminally involved youth.

Moments later the summer moon escaped from behind the clouds, exposing our dark clothing to the drug addicted customers who frequented our city block.

Then suddenly from the opposite side of this busy street, I heard the base-filled voice of Rome, yelling from a money green Honda.

"Come take a ride wit me; Fat Tah, come on!"

Rome was a thirty year veteran of street life, who employed dozens of teenage youth to distribute cocaine on the street where I lived. He had a reputation of being a heartless murderer, as well as possessing a low tolerance for disobedience.

After responding with a head nod, my ashy fist tightened, to connect with the fist of my curly haired co-worker Dre.

Now, Dre was seventeen years old like myself and was known to be extremely sociable, unlike me. Dre was raised by his hardworking grandmother, following the heroin related death of both his parents.

Oddly on that night, Dre hardly spoke a word, but what was most weird was his repeated smoking of cigarettes. Dre wasn't a chain smoker, but part of me figured he was trying to cope with yesterday's murder of our friend Rodney.

Rodney sold crack just like Dre and me, but unfortunately was shot to death while working in one of Rome's crack houses.

Throughout the day and up until that night I still hadn't digested the horrific murder of Rodney, but I figured his brother Rome was suffering way more than me.

As a strong presence of guilt strangled my thoughts, I crossed the street inhaling cool air as I entered the car.

"Daaag Fat Tah, I'm happy to see that you finally wobbled over here!" Rome angrily, said.

"Yeah man, I just got rid of my last bag!"

Hidden behind tinted windows, we slowly pulled off as the broken steering column and absence of keys in the ignition became very obvious to me.

It wasn't uncommon for me to ride in stolen vehicles, but what really concerned me were my feelings of anger and guilt related to Rodney's murder.

I felt guilty because I knew valuable information about

that bloody night, but in the streets we feared the consequences of talking to police.

Realizing I had no one else to talk to, I figured my next best option would be to inform Rome.

After a few seconds of gathering my thoughts, I caught a glimpse of Rome's boney hands, noticing a pair of black gloves glued to his matching skin.

"I go away for a few days and somebody goes and kills my lil' brotha, just like dat! For real man, who ever did it, is gonna pay!"

"I'm not sure, but..."

"But what Fat Tah, if you know something you need to say it!"

Throughout my childhood, I heard about and witnessed Rome's violence, which I knew was going to be the result of whatever statement I provided.

So I began to think back to the night of Rodney's murder , possibly due to fear of Rome's short temper, but mostly because Rome was my employer and Rodney's only brother.

As those feelings of indebtedness circulated through my veins, I prepared to speak, not knowing I would forever regret what followed.

"It was three dudes, two of them wore masks and the third person was bare face. The person with no mask was a young boy like me and I've seen him hustlin in front of the Chinese store."

"The Chinese store around the corner!" Rome yelled, as if it was unbelievable.

"Yeah, right dere."

"Oh hell no! Who else did you tell this to?"

"Nobody!"

"Well if you seen the people, why didn't you do something?"

"I couldn't, the gun you gave me got stolen!" I yelled.

Feeling as if I was being disciplined by a parent, my

chubby body sunk deeper into the passenger seat, as air raced out of my nostrils.

"My fault Fat Tah, I don't mean to take this out on you, it's just I lost my lil' bro and I always looked at you as my other lil' bro, so I expect great things out of you. Plus, I heard somebody else talkin bout dis young dude over by the Chinese store, so I know both of y'all ain't lying."

For the next thirty minutes Rome drove through the pothole infested streets of Camden, as I continued to explain what happened.

"On that night, the gunshots woke me out of my sleep and when I looked out into the alley, I saw three people running out of the house where Rodney was working. I went to grab my gun, but it wasn't where I left it."

Without warning we drove past the Chinese store, as Rome searched the dismal scenery for the young suspect.

"Maaan forget all that explaining stuff, that's the young boy right dere I think?"

"Yeah, yeah Rome that's him right there, leaning against the wall, counting money!"

With eyes focused to kill, Rome reached underneath his seat and placed a dark colored revolver on my lap.

"This is yours now, so watch my back while I go handle this situation!"

As Rome circled the block one last time, I could feel the souls of countless bodies weighing down the steel object.

For some reason my chubby palms began to sweat with nervousness and out of nowhere I had a flashback about being choked by rough hands.

As I returned from my brief thoughts, the car stereo echoed the words "My Mind's Playin Tricks on Me," but at that time I didn't think of it as a message.

"Look, this is what has to be done!" Rome explained, as if he could detect my reluctant feelings.

6

"Yeah, I gottcha!"

With his automatic weapon, now removed from his waist, Rome parked the tinted vehicle directly in front of the Chinese store, as I relocated the revolver to the pocket of my hoodie.

"Showtime Fat Daddy!"

"I-I-I'm not ready for this!" I nervously mumbled.

"Yo, you soundin like some scared little boy, who ain't ready to become a man!"

Feeling Rome's expectations begin to overshadow my own, I exited the car, draping a tobacco scented hood over my head.

Nevertheless, Rome moved with Olympic speed as he walked toward the side of the Chinese store to meet his victim.

Confused in thought about the consequences of bad decisions, I sprinted as fast as I could, in the opposite direction of Rome.

While running with fear weighing heavy on my heart, I noticed that the moon was shining brighter than normal, as if GOD was opening his eyes to watch me.

Then suddenly, my burst of energy came to an end, as I heard the roar of three loud gun shots coming from the direction of the Chinese store.

At that moment, I escaped to a dark alley behind our hangout spot, Felipe's Bodega, remembering when I saw a ten year old boy dead with bloodstained jewelry around his neck.

I think it was the saddest picture this neighborhood had ever seen, as the child's lifeless body was found behind Felipe's holding a sandwich bag full of crack cocaine.

Scared and worried as police sirens echoed from a distance, I ducked behind Felipe's dumpster, as a dark colored car with no lights entered the alley.

At first, I had no idea who was driving the car, hearing a childish giggle as the car got closer.

"I know you don't think all that blubber can fit behind that dumpster, Fat Tah!" Rome laughed.

"Who told you I was back here?" I asked, as my palms warmed the freezing gun.

"Some crackheads saw you, but anyway come here!"

Quickly directing my attention toward Rome's every movement, I walked toward the car, still clutching the small weapon.

"I guess you wondering why I ran away!"

"Look, I already know you ain't no killer, but I think with the right training, you'll be ready in no time!" Rome said, as a fog of weed smoke exited the car.

"Yeah Rome, I guess you're right!"

Although it was difficult to mentally absorb everything Rome was saying, I continued to stare at my skinny boss, as his murderous hands signaled for me to get into the car.

Once I entered the stolen Honda, my heart pounded like police knocks, as I wiped away sweat from my oval-shaped head.

While arguing with my conscious about making smart decisions, I wondered if the young boy Rome just shot, was suffering from the same peer pressure that I've been experiencing.

"Hey Fat Tah, you wanna smoke some of this weed?"

"Naw you got it, I'm gonna smoke a cigarette."

Rome continued to exhale smoke through his wide nose, as we remained parked in the dark alley behind Felipe's Bodega.

"Tonight I'm gonna need you to wobble ya chubby butt back to work, so I want you to meet up with E-Ward, so he can give you what you need."

"Cool!" I said, as Rome's lanky hands suddenly grabbed my arm.

"Remember, everything ain't for everybody's ears!" Rome bluntly stated.

"I understand." I said, while exiting the smoke filled car.

After shutting the door, I watched the car disappear into the darkness, as I walked as fast as I could in the direction of my house.

I used that time alone to think of positive reasons for living this life I was given, but those reasons seemed to always be unrealistic.

In my mind everything I did was justified by tragic memories that raped my happiness day and night. I wondered if I was destined to keep dealing with my untold experiences alone, but also I wanted to identify who the real me was.

Finally I reached my deceased grandmother's two-story row home, greeted by the scent of lingering cigarette smoke as I entered.

My footsteps seemed to echo throughout this empty house as I jogged up the wooden stairs, surprised that my mom's room light was on.

"Hey mom, mom, wake up!"

Her skeleton-like frame rolled over as her brown eyes opened with redness to accompany a raspy tone.

"Whaat, whaaat, what the hell do you want Fat Tah?"

"Mom, what did you do wit my gun?"

"First off, leeet me remind you, because you be forgettin this stuff, anything in mama's house, is ma-ma's, plus mama don't like guns. Uhmm hum, that's right."

As she returned to her sleep, I shook my head from side to side, realizing we had been down this road in the past.

For the next five minutes I stood with her mattress at my feet, wishing we had a clear understanding of each other, but she was always too high off of crack and I was too lost in anger.

While exiting her room and entering my own, I suddenly remembered the explosive echo of Rome's automatic weapon.

I wasn't sure if I felt remorse or if I cared whether I was the next to die a violent death, but I foolishly thought it didn't really matter.

In the street life, it seemed as if everyone around me was obsessed with violence, whether it was the music they listened too, the movies they watched or the way they handled conflict.

Realizing that I wasn't going to be the person to think differently, I quickly changed my clothes hearing a sorrowful cry from outside my bedroom window.

"Ohhh Goddd, why my baaaby, whhhhy!"

When I looked out my window into the back of my house, I noticed that the alley was candle lit with a large crowd of people gathered.

At the front of this crowd was Rodney's teary eyed mom, Ms. Douglas smothering two large baby photos with her sausage like hands.

For a quick moment, my brown eyes stared into the night sky, wondering if Rodney's soul actually found peace or at least some form of happiness.

While attempting to ignore the parade of countless memories, I exited the house instantly blending in with the large crowd.

As usual there were older guys from the block, along with teenage boys and girls who were placing balloons, teddy bears, and liquor bottles in front of the house where Rodney was murdered.

Although I knew all the tears in the world couldn't bring Rodney back to life, I could feel that change was needed, especially while watching Poddy Pod, a former school teacher turned crack addict, search through trash cans for food.

People from all around the neighborhood continued to crowd the alley, but I was mainly surprised by the absence of Mr. Gilliam, the so called block captain. He was always giving one of his "save the community" speeches, especially during times like this.

Even though, his speeches were lengthy and normally spoke against crime, I couldn't help but understand why people respected him so much.

"Fat Tah, why can't you and the rest of these boys around here be like other kids y'all age?" Ms. Douglas asked, while wobbling toward my direction.

I didn't have a proper answer for Ms. Douglas's question because we were doing what most kids our age were doing, especially kids in this neighborhood, plus her oldest son Rome, was the guy we worked for.

"Ms. Douglas I don't know what's going on or why dis even happened!" I said, while removing a cigarette from my pocket.

Ms. Douglas continued to blame my friends and me for her son's death, which made me realize that Ms. Douglas was clueless about Rodney, because everyone knew that Rodney was working for his brother Rome.

"As a young boy, my son wanted to be an athlete and worked hard to get good grades, but placed his dreams aside in order to live out the dreams of you and the rest of those heartless thugs down at that store! I raised both of my sons all by myself and did the best for them without help from anybody. Heee was myyyy baaaby!"

Watching a crying and angered Ms. Douglas drop to her flabby knees, made me think about the pain all parents must feel when losing a child to violence.

Realizing I needed a change of scenery before the situation worsened, I slowly exited the candle lit alley as the moon's camera followed.

While traveling through the connecting alleys, I saw a reflection of me in each abandoned house I passed, realizing they had a body with a lost soul, just like me.

As I got closer to my worksite, I could see the colorful mural painted on Felipe's Bodega, of my friend E-Ward's little brother and sister.

About two years ago, they were both shot to death during a robbery at Felipe's and during that period of time, nobody knew who did it.

When I arrived at Felipe's, I greeted E-Ward with a hug, placing the money I earned for Rome earlier that night, into E-Ward's jacket pocket.

E-Ward was a twenty-year old street soldier, who had been selling drugs on this block since he was nine years old. E-Ward's main responsibilities now, was to collect the money and make sure all workers were supplied with drugs.

After breaking the hug, E-Ward reversed his fitted hat, as his short frame leaned against the wall of Felipe's.

"So what's been up E-Wizzy?" I asked.

"Coolin baby, yo, you know I heard that your boy was up in the crack house when Rodney got killed the other night!"

"Who are you talkin about?"

"Ya boy Dre, that's who!" E-Ward said, with bulging eyes.

"Naw Dre would never let something like that happen to Rodney."

"If you say so, my fat friend."

"I'm sayin..."

"You're saying what; just ask yourself why didn't Dre get shot, but Rodney did, coincidence, I guess! Look man; let me go get that stuff for you, before I get upset!"

E-Ward's stocky frame exited the block as I continued to replay our conversation throughout my mind. It seemed the more thought I gave it, the more rage bubbled inside of me.

After standing frozen in thought, I quickly walked into Felipe's ordering me a sandwich with extra meat.

As I exited the store with my sandwich in hand, I saw Dre leaning into the window of a gray Ford. Uncertain if Dre was making a sale to what looked like undercover cops, I waited until the car pulled off before I did anything.

While taking large bites out of my meaty sandwich, I walked toward Dre watching his yellow face, darken with nervousness.

"I thought you were done for the night!" Dre said, while counting the money from his sale.

"Yo, I think the people you just served were cops!"

"Naw man you crazy, they just some dudes from da suburbs looking for crack!"

Feeling my emotions get the best of me, I knew I had to bring up any questions I had about the murder.

"Question, my boy, was you in the crack house when Rodney got shot up?"

"C'mon Fat Tah, why you asking me something like that?"

"'Cause you been acting real strange!" I said, while eating the last of my sandwich.

Dre pulled his black hood over his curly hair, as his slender frame leaned against the traffic pole.

"Take a hike somewhere man, cause you keep asking me questions like you my girl or somethin!"

CHAPTER

2

At that moment E-Ward drove past us in a burgundy Pontiac, pointing his stubby fingers in the direction of the alley.

I desperately wanted to punch Dre in his mouth, but I needed to grab my supply from E-Ward before I did anything.

"Trust me, you gonna get yours pretty boy!"

"Whatever you say, Fat Tah!"

I quickly entered the dark alley to receive my assignment, leaving E-Ward with words of "Peace," before he drove off.

After stashing the drugs in an abandoned car, I kept about three bags of crack in my pocket, since traffic seemed slower than usual.

When I returned to the storefront, Felipe's had closed for the night, as I stood patiently searching for Dre.

Within seconds I found him standing in front of an

abandoned house, serving drugs to loyal customers.

Still focused on some form of revenge, I thought back on Dre's slick talk and plotted my attack.

So I walked across the street and without mumbling a word I connected a right hook to his fleshless jaw. Dre instantly fell against the graffiti stained porch of this house, with his brown eyes closed shut.

"Wow baby boy!" A shirtless customer yelled out.

Watching Dre attempt to get himself together, I asked the man, "How many?"

"I-I-I wanted to know if I could get three for fifty-five."

I was willing to take the short, so I served the customer, while watching Dre behave like a coward and walk to the other end of the block.

In my mind I didn't know what to expect next, so I decided to relocate close to where my stash was at.

As my jeans sagged, I walked in the shadows of the block, hearing the hunger of the night-sky rumble with thunder.

After about ten minutes of hanging in this gloomy environment, I was approached by E-Ward's mom and dad, who were desperately in need of crack.

Mrs. Tomons repeatedly rubbed her skinny hands along her diamond shaped face, as she approached in my direction.

I remembered when she and Mr. Tomons were responsible parents, but seemed to lose a grip when their two youngest children got killed inside of Felipe's. Although I wanted and needed the money, I refused to disrespect my relationship with E-Ward.

"Fat Tah, you holdin, baby?" she asked.

"Naw, ain't nothing out here right now."

Mr. Tomon's lanky frame, motioned impatiently, as he stood with a forty ounce of beer in his hand.

"Well, how long we gotta wait Fat Tah?" Mr. Tomon's asked.

"Like, fifteen or twenty minutes."

Mrs. Tomons delivered a look of disbelief, while fixing her bra strap from underneath her dingy white T-shirt.

"I know you holdin something, 'cause you ain't got no other reason to be standing ya big ass out here!" Mrs. Tomon's yelled.

"For real auntee, ain't nothing out here right now!"

Mrs. Tomons knew I had drugs on me, so she even tried rubbing her hand on my chubby stomach.

"C'monnn, what a girl gotta do?"

Instantly I pushed her hands off of my stomach as the smell of cigarettes and malt-liquor entered my nose.

"C'mon ma, you like family to me!" I boastfully said.

"Uh hum, uh hum, family, well forget family and forget you, you fat bastard!"

Breathing a short sigh of relief, as Mr. and Mrs. Tomons exited the block, I realized I was going to have that same conversation with them, every half hour until my shift ended.

As minimal traffic drove down the block, I heard the booming sounds of a shotgun blast, from a distance. After hearing the shots, I realized the only people I had to watch my back, were crack addicted police lookouts.

Despite my worries, I stood underneath the yellow awning of Felipe's Bodega, as cash paying customers appeared, while others tried to exchange stolen items for drugs.

Surrounded by these pain and stress driven clients I suddenly heard their speechless cry for help, realizing we were both chasing heaven with the reality of hell shackled to our brains. "If only air could bleed," I thought to myself.

Unfortunately, memories of my childhood started to surface, as thunder rumbled the dark sky, making me wonder if GOD was crying just as I wanted to.

Somehow losing this daily battle, a few tears escaped the corners of my eyes, quickly met by a gang of soothing raindrops.

Although my clothes were soaking wet after selling almost two thousand dollars worth of crack cocaine, the rain eventually came to an end.

Then suddenly from a short distance, I noticed the hooded frame and muscular strut of Big Ede approaching in my direction.

Big Ede was a ruthless neighborhood legend, who had control of this block, until the DEA arrested him and his entire team of workers, about eleven years ago. Big Ede served about ten years in Federal Prison and is now back on the streets trying to reclaim what he lost.

"Hey youngin I'm out here now, so take whatever you got somewhere else!" Big Ede demanded.

Usually it's about three or four young boys working on the graveyard shift, with E-Ward supervising, but on this particular night it was only me, Dre and a couple of crack addicted lookouts to watch for police.

Maintaining my cool, I ignored the tough talk, remembering the small weapon Rome gave me.

"It's cool, I'm about to get out of here anyway." I said while watching Big Ede's every movement.

Big Ede nodded his head with agreement, revealing a village of razor bumps, as he placed a cheap cigar in the corner of his mouth.

"Hey youngin, give me your money so I can take it to Rome!"

It seemed as if a bell rung in my head telling me to wake up. So, I quickly placed my right hand underneath my hoodie, wrapping my palms around the loaded weapon.

"Big Ede, I ain't got no money to give you?" I sarcastically said.

With a blank stare in his glassy eyes, Big Ede started to reach inside the pocket of his hoodie.

"This is my block out here and will always be!" Big Ede shouted with anger.

"Two black and whites comin down!" one of the lookouts

yelled.

Not even a second later, the lookout on the opposite end of the block yelled, "Suburban comin down!"

At that moment I knew we were about to get raided by the police, so I sprinted into the dark alley, quickly separating myself from Big Ede. Then out of nowhere the rain started to pour again, as I ran inside of an abandoned house, fearful of being arrested for the third time in three years.

After exiting onto another street, I attempted to keep my balance while cautiously running along rain drenched sidewalks, taking advantage of limited escape routes.

Unwilling to spend another six months in juvenile detention, I quickly slid underneath a newer model Chrysler, as police lights illuminated the streets.

After about twenty minutes of lying in a puddle of oil and water, I was determined to try and make it home.

During my walk beneath the light gray sky, I talked with GOD seeking understanding to help me clearly see my purpose in life, especially since I was quickly losing faith with nobody positive around me.

Hearing police sirens in close distance, I quickly entered my basement through a squeaky wooden door, only to be greeted by the sight of my skinny short-haired mom, holding a small pipe to her mouth.

Startled by my untimely entrance, she dropped the glass object, shouting profanity as her buggy eyes expanded with anger.

"Where was your fat ass at?" she asked, while reaching for a wooden broom.

In an attempt to create some common ground and keep her from swinging the broom at me, I played the sorry role.

"Mom I'm sorry, I didn't know you were down here, but anyway what you doing?"

"Don't ever question what I do or where I be at!" she yelled.

Holding the wooden broom with her right hand, she pointed toward the basement steps.

"Matta fact let mama hold a couple dollars, before you take ya fat ass upstairs!"

Attempting to ignore her, I walked toward the stairs stepping over piles of dirty clothes.

"Mom you know what you're gonna do with the money, so just go lay down and try to get some sleep!"

"Oh you gonna tell me what to do, like you know my life or somethin, you ungrateful bastard! Remember you still live in the house, my parents slaved for, so don't ever forget it!"

In my mind I just wanted to tell her that she's my heart and that I wanted her to get some help, so that we could live like a regular family, but honestly I didn't really know what a regular family was like and plus I just didn't know how to tell her my feelings.

"Mom, I'm tired of you actin like everything in our house is cool, or like I see you every day or like I know where you be at all the time!   Or..."

"You ungrateful bastard!"

Were the last words I heard, before every part of my body was hit with the wooden broom, eventually causing it to break apart.

After a few minutes of this beating, I grabbed the wooden stick from her hand while delivering a deep stare, feeling blood leak from the back of my head.

Really unsure of what to expect next, I sprinted up the stairs to my room, in order to escape her angered presence.

As I entered my room, I quickly closed the door and used my lopsided bed to barricade myself in the room.

From behind my door I could hear her footsteps traveling up the squeaky stairs, but to my surprise she avoided any attempts to enter my room. Happy about her decision, but feeling the weight of the whole world on my shoulders I quietly let out a sea of salty tears.

For the next five minutes I used one of my dirty T-Shirt's to catch my downpour as well as the leaking blood, exiting the back of my head. Still crying and overwhelmed by my life, I eventually fell into an unwanted sleep.

While barricaded in this room, my chubby body moaned and shook as I dreamt about the events of my ninth birthday.

On that day my mom and two of her girlfriends came to our house to help her celebrate my birthday. They danced and played Stevie Wonder albums on my deceased grandmother's record player, as I ate food from the Chinese store.

After about two hours of this small party, my mom and her girlfriends decided to walk to Felipe's to so-called "get something."

As my mom and her friends walked out the door, she told me that she was leaving the door unlocked because she was coming right back.

Since I was alone, I decided to go upstairs and take a nap, but when I heard the front door open, a deep toned voice was yelling, "Happy Birthday Fat Tah!"

I immediately recognized the voice, as fear traveled throughout my nine year-old body. So my first thought was to stay positioned in my room, especially after hearing him shut and lock the front door.

"Come downstairs Fat Tah!" he requested.

It seemed as if my throat was clogged with peanut butter, as I foolishly walked down the wooden stairs, only to be greeted by a closed fist punch to the face. At that, moment a combination of snot and tears begun to flow as I fell to the hardwood floor, quickly crawling underneath my mom's card table.

While moving at light's speed with an unstoppable look of hunger in his eyes, this beast chased me around the house connecting about three more breath-taking punches to my body.

I was terrified and aching as I fell to the floor once again, which allowed him to forcefully pull my pants and underwear off my weakened body. The strong grip and aggressiveness of this adult man, allowed him to position me face down on the floor, as no words or screams exited my mouth.

Celebrating his unbeaten record, this beast grunted and sighed as each forceful motion penetrated my innocence, once again.

Suddenly I awoke, as the morning sunlight greeted my crust-filled eyes, hearing the continual honks from a car horn echoing in the air.

The person honking the horn was yelling something, but I couldn't understand it, so after about another two minutes of this madness, I approached my bedroom window.

After removing the fan from my paint chipped window, I paused for a second, trying to ignore the paranoid thoughts still dancing in my head.

Although there may be obvious answers for every problem, I was clueless and needed someone to help erase those memories, before I made an irreversible decision.

Wiping sweat from my chubby forehead, I looked out of the window, recognizing Murray's rectangular head, yelling out of a red Cadillac.

Murray was an eighteen year old friend of mine, who was a known car thief and employee of Rome. Murray's mother died while giving birth to him and since then he has been raised by his father Mr. Gilliam, the block captain. Although Mr. Gilliam is a positive role model, Murray preferred to model himself after Rome.

"Daaag Fat Tah, you too young to be playing with yourself already!" Murray yelled out.

"Yeah, your aunt was giving me a shower, but we'll be done in a minute!"

"C'mon maaan, don't be takin forever, because it's

police all around here!" Murray pleaded.

I removed the barricade from my door and walked toward the bathroom, noticing that my mom was absent as usual.

After quickly getting dressed, I put my gun underneath my white T-shirt and grabbed Rome's money.

When I exited my house, Murray greeted me with his caramel colored hands, as the shine from the stolen Cadillac almost blinded me.

"Murray, your big ass is crazy! You must really take probation as a joke!"

"Look baby, I seen my P.O. yesterday and this is the machine that took me there!" Murray boastfully explained.

"You a wild dude, cuz I don't ever wanna have to see the inside of a probation office again!"

For the next hour or two, we drove the stolen car through almost every section of the city, blasting rap songs from the past and present, as Murray and I blew kisses at passing women.

Unfortunately, past memories of Rodney started to flash in my head as I looked over at his picture, air-brushed on Murray's T-shirt.

"I was surprised that your dad didn't come and make a speech the other night when everybody was in the alley."

Smiling as if he had hit the lottery, Murray pulled a rolled blunt from out of his left ear.

"My dad told me, that he was probably gonna somethin at the funeral tomorrow, but anyway why did Ms. Douglas start blaming you for Rodney's murder."

"I guess she was yelling at me because Rodney was always with us, or maybe she just didn't know who to take her anger out on... man I really don't know!"

While searching for another CD to put in the radio, I opened the glove compartment only to be greeted by several sandwich bags full of crack cocaine.

Instantly feeling more hot lava spill into the car, I realized I wasn't willing to risk being locked up again, especially under those circumstances. So, I smoked a few cigarettes to relax my thoughts, while Murray's dark colored lips exhaled weed smoke.

"Yo Murray, take me back to da block, so I can talk to E-Ward about somethin."

"C'mon baby, you over there shaking in your boots, matta fact, here hit this weed!"

CHAPTER

3

About twenty minutes later we arrived in front of the painted mural of E-Ward's sister and brother, hearing the loud mouth of Rome's dreadlock wearing partner Cuk, who was rolling dice in front of Felipe's.

Cuk was a twenty-eight year old, short tempered street veteran, who had been a former high school football star, until being shot in the knee. Cuk was Rome's right hand man, but was known in the streets as being very untrustworthy.

"Wuuuuu weee, ain't nutin like new monay, ain't-nuttin like it, I tell ya, I tell ya!" Cuk yelled at the top of his lungs.

After completely exiting the car and reminding Murray to "stay safe," my attention was grabbed by the sight of a sparkling gray Benz Coupe, with large sized rims, double parked in front of Felipe's.

The blinking hazard lights on this vehicle seemed like

the New Year's countdown to gunfire, because every dice game ended just about the same, either somebody was shot, robbed or beat-up badly.

So basically, all I could do was squeeze into a front row view and patiently await the obvious, as a fog of weed smoke surrounded Cuk and the rest of Rome's disciples.

Minutes passed along with the dice, as trash talking increased, large amounts of cash resting on the concrete, did as well. By this time the two main participants of the dice game were Cuk and an extremely dark colored man. The extremely dark colored man wore a gold chain and danced after each roll, as if the blazing sun was a spotlight and the sidewalk his stage.

Apparently this dancing fool was good with dice, which was noticeable by the amount of money bulging out each of his of pockets.

I wasn't really sure of who this dancing fool was, but I knew winning that amount of money off of this block wasn't good, especially if you weren't respected or even known in this neighborhood.

As freshly washed cars blasting loud music drove slowly through the block, I no longer concerned myself with the fate of Cuk's opponent, but instantly became aroused by the rotating presence of sweet scented females, making their guest appearance on the block.

Although my lustful thoughts remained unspoken, many of the small money spectators, who entertained side bets, were shouting smooth greetings and attempting to buy love.

Uninterested in the presence of beautiful females, there were also other spectators who drooled like wolves at the opportunity to rob somebody, especially somebody with fat pockets and wearing a chain as massive as the one on Cuk's opponent.

As I directed my attention back on the dice game, Cuk's opponent was smiling with teeth as bright as the gold chain around his neck.

"Wow, I just love the hospitality around here, y'all just brought me new rims for my Benz. Maaaan, I need to come get a piece of this money every day!"

After hearing that statement, the nearby traffic light changed from red to green as the small circle of spectators seemed to tighten.

While smiling behind thick dreadlocks, Cuk extended a handshake to his opponent, while almost unnoticeably delivering a head nod to one of the salivating spectators, huddled in the crowd.

"Well good brotha, it's been real!" Cuk sarcastically said.

"Yes sirrr, it has! But look if y'all fellas is gonna be given away money, oh, I mean doing this again, anytime soon, you can give me a call. Matta fact I'll go to my car and write my cell number down for you!"

As this dark colored man attempted to exit the circle, he was met by a knee buckling right hook that sent him directly to the warm concrete.

The bearded individual who delivered the punch, drooled with hunger as he emptied the pockets of the fallen man, returning all money back to Cuk.

Cuk smiled while placing the money in his pocket, as his blood thirsty hit-man kept the car keys and snatched the dark colored man's gold chain.

Cuk crumbled a five dollar bill into a ball, bouncing it off of the face of the dark colored man.

"Hey tar baby, uhh make sure you leave that number for me alright! Oh yeah here's five, so that you can get back to wherever you from!"

As blood leaked like a faucet from the mouth of the fallen man, he seemed as if he was seeking some type of understanding, while watching Cuk exit the circle.

"Why does it have to be like this?" he softly pleaded.

Watching as the tar colored man attempted to stand on his feet, Cuk's bearded hit-man laughed as if somebody told a joke, while delivering three field goal style kicks, to the face of the dark colored man.

"Lay down! Nobody told you to get up! You gonna lay here until these females walking by, feel sorry for your punk ass and help you up!" The bearded hit-man yelled.

As this bloody faced man sat with his back against the mural of E-Ward's brother and sister, it seemed as if their painted brown eyes, were crying the tears of every community praying for peace.

Seconds later, the huddled crowd of dice shooters started to exit in separate directions, as I attempted to get away from the corner before the police showed up.

Glancing back at the fallen stranger, I walked along thirsty sidewalks, which patiently awaited the blood of the next homicide victim.

Realizing, that my eyes were opening wider to the problems plaguing my community, I instantly saw a reflection of myself on a passing car, which quickly disappeared, with the blink of my eyes.

Those thoughts seemed to take a back seat, as I was greeted by the sneaky chipped tooth smile of Rome, driving a blue Jeep Grande Cherokee with Cuk riding shotgun.

Showing no care for the ongoing traffic, Rome stopped the jeep as if he owned the world, while lowering his window with a smile on his skinny face.

"I'm willing to bet fifty dollars that you just lost three pounds, walking from Felipe's to here!"

Moving the dreadlocks out of his pie shaped face, Cuk leaned across Rome adding his comments.

"Mannn forget fifty dollars, I'll bet you a hundred, because that chunky monkey been sweating since he stepped foot in the dice game!"

Smiling as the sound of car horns increased, I walked across the street feeling the community's eyes watching.

"Yo, y'all gonna stop with those fat jokes, for real, because Cuk you only a honey bun away from a diet, and Rome I think I just sent some money over to your country yesterday!"

Suddenly Rome nodded his head for me to get in, as he quickly increased the volume of his radio.

When I got in the jeep, I was immediately met by the aroma of vanilla scented air fresheners and weed smoke, hearing the license plate rattle, from music exiting the speakers.

As the jeep circled the block I could feel the soft leather seats, cool my heated body, while Rome attempted to shout over the music exiting the radio.

"I hope both of y'all greasy chunks of lard, wiped y'all feet before sittin in my truck! Please tell me y'all did, because I would hate to kick somebody out in that heat, but I'll do it!"

As sounds of laughter exited the mouth of Cuk's and mine, Rome continued to drive, while bopping his skinny head to the musical beats.

We all seemed to be enjoying the ride, watching barely dressed females, walk the neighborhood looking for money making saviors, while Rome verbalized jokes about females not meeting his standards.

In good spirits, our neighborhood tour continued, but changed as we drove past the most beautiful girl I've ever known to push a baby stroller. It was Cuk's younger sister Talianna, who was wearing extremely tight shorts, and a blue half shirt, revealing her undamaged figure.

"Whoa, whoa, whoa, Rome stop da car!" Cuk demanded.

Cuk hopped out the jeep and ran toward his silky haired sister, as if he were an undercover cop, instantly grabbing her arm.

"Talianna, where do you think you going, dressed like dat!"

"First of all, you ain't my dad, last time I checked my

dad was in Trenton State Prison, serving life! But if your simple ass really needs to know where I'm going, I'm going to my baby dad mom's house!"

Talianna's hazel eyes filled with tears as she fixed her hair, tied in a ponytail.

"Last night my baby dad was killed outside of the Chinese store, around the corner, so now I'm on my way to his mom's house to see what they gonna do about his funeral."

Cuk lifted the newborn baby out of the stroller, kissing the fatherless child on the head.

"Look lil sis, I'm sorry bout what happened, but don't worry everything is gonna be alright, trust me. Here take this money so that you can call a cab, when you leave his mom's house."

Cuk walked back to the jeep, while I adored Talianna's beauty, as she tucked the money into the tight pockets of her shorts.

For a moment I got lost in thought, thinking back to when we were close friends; until the news of her pregnancy, which upset me. I was mad because I didn't know who she was having a baby by, but most of all she was my first real crush as well as my first true friend.

While back in the jeep, Cuk was speechless for a couple of minutes, until he reached into the pockets of his linen shorts pulling out a clear bag of weed and a small pack of white wrapping paper.

"Damn, I didn't even know that was my lil' sis baby dad, who got killed last night!"

Rome's skinny frame leaned back further in the seat, using his left hand as a cushion for his head, while keeping the other on the steering wheel.

"That's some crazy stuff, for real. These young boys keep dying, because they need real men in their lives. Ain't that right, Fat Tah." Rome sarcastically said.

"Yeah, I guess so," I replied.

Cuk was clueless, as he started to separate the neon colored weed on a CD case, but seemed to need another ingredient as he tapped Rome on the arm.

"Hey Rome, stop playing around man!"

Rome smiled as he tossed two small bags of cocaine into Cuk's lap, singing happily while changing the CD.

"Ain't nuthin like da real thing baa-be, ain't nuthin like da reeal thing!"

Cuk laughed, while rolling the combination of drugs into a thin white stick, hearing Rome continue on with his singing.

After finishing his project, Cuk's dreadlock covered face, turned in my direction.

"Youngin you smoking yet?" Cuk invitingly asked.

"No thank you brotha, I only smoke "Ports"!"

Rome instantly stopped singing, to deliver another one of his short speeches.

"Look Fat Tah, you my lil' bro and all, but I don't allow no cigarette smoke in my car, now weed smoke, yeah, but no cigarettes, ports, or whatever you wanna call'em!"

I smiled, as Rome adjusted the air conditioner and began smoking with Cuk.

"Fat Tah, I want you to listen to what I'm bout to say, alright!"

"Damn Rome, what is it now!" I replied

"Look, I only want you to make decisions that'll help you grab your little piece of heaven, understand me, but if your everyday all-day is heaven, you probably grabbed too much!"

Embracing the lit object as Rome passed it in my direction, I was tempted to place my lips on it, but quickly passed it to Cuk.

At that moment I wondered if my mom's addiction started this way, but I also remembered the night Murray beat a pregnant woman, for buying crack with a fake twenty-dollar bill.

Cuk quickly lowered the lit object, as we drove toward a gang of Camden City Police cars, parked with their overhead lights flashing.

"A yo Rome, ain't that your clone with the handcuffs on!" Cuk said, as he exhaled a small cloud of smoke.

Murray was face down on the hood of that red Cadillac with a silver colored handgun and several sandwich bags of crack cocaine scattered next to him.

Angered by Murray's stupidity Rome silenced the radio, while smacking his skinny hand on the steering wheel.

"No common sense, not one drop of common sense is in that boy's head!" Rome angrily stated.

"Well brotha Rome, just take the loss on the chin and lets continue to do what we do best...Get Money!" Cuk interjected.

Continuing to maintain a moderate driving speed, we passed the arresting officers avoiding any unnecessary eye contact.

The quietness that followed was scary, but what made it worse was that for the first time in my life, I started to seriously think about my future. I wasn't sure of anything, but I knew in my heart that losing my freedom, shouldn't be an option.

Rome turned the radio back on, but kept it at a very low volume, as drug dealing messages surfed across the air waves.

At that moment, I wondered if anyone else in the car was thinking the same as I was. I decided to look into the rearview mirror only to be greeted by Rome's devilish eyes, but amazed at the redness of Cuk's, as he sat quietly looking out of the window.

Suddenly the monotony was broken, as my chubby body flinched to the sound of Rome's pager, vibrating on the dashboard.

"Fat Tah, you alright back dere?" Rome asked.

"Yeah, I'm good baby!"

Rome continued to drive as he read the message on

his pager.

"A-yo Cuk, wake up and let me know if you see a pay phone on your side!"

Cuk's tattooed hands squeezed into his pockets, pulling out a cell phone, but Rome quickly shook his head with disagreement.

"Mannn, go ahead and use my cell phone and get rid of dat pager, for God's sake!" Cuk demanded.

"Look nappy dreads, just let me know if you see a pa…, never mind it's one right here."

Rome parked at a nearby store, quickly exiting the jeep.

As Rome talked on the pay phone, he kept his slender back against the wall, constantly moving his twiggy fingers, as if he were giving orders or directing traffic.

While awaiting Rome's return, Cuk called someone from his cell phone, telling them our exact location, even down to the address of the store. This was odd to me, although I wasn't sure as to how Rome and Cuk conducted their business.

For the next two or three minutes, Cuk talked on his cell phone as I victoriously fought the temptation to smoke a cigarette.

Returning back to this mysterious conversation in front of me, I remained clueless as to who Cuk was talking too, and why he said the things that he said. Then suddenly the words "I love you," exited Cuk's mouth, as he hung up the phone.

CHAPTER

4

Unable to hold back my laugh I said, "I love youuu! Ha, Haaa!"

Cuk appeared to be annoyed by my comment, as he opened the passenger side door, using his thick hands to shake ashes off of his linen shirt.

"A yo, let me tell you something. Whoever tells you they don't love nobody, they a straight up liar. And just for your information Fatlock Holmes, I always tell my mom I love her, no matter what!"

The driver side door slammed as Rome sat behind the steering wheel, with a frustrated look glued to his narrow face.

"Fat Tah, I'm about to take a drive, so I'll probably drop you off at Felipe's."

Somehow the cool scented air failed to freeze my sweat, as I nervously wondered what was about to unfold.

"Hey Rome, I can walk from here and I'll catch up with y'all later."

Sensing a fierce presence of mystery within the jeep, I quickly made my exit hearing no departing words from either Rome or Cuk.

Regretting that I had declined Rome's offer, I instantly felt the arms of humidity wrapped around my lungs.

Utilizing long steps and deep breaths, I eventually got closer to my destination, as beads of sweat raced down the crease of my chubby back, reloading yet another memory into my mental gun.

"I can't loose another day of my life, I can't, I just can't do it!" I thought to myself.

But despite my efforts to block those memories, I remembered the day I begged for immunity as my predator nourished his sickness, once again.

He normally achieved his goal, but on that particular day he made sure of it. That day I had locked myself in my room, but to my surprise his adult strength was so overpowering that he broke my bedroom door off of its hinges.

In clear sight of harm, fear closed my brown eyes, which scared my feeble heart to the point of not fighting.

Today made another day that I couldn't understand why I was such a perfect target, especially to another male. But my main question every day was, "Did I ever ask him to do the life-changing things that he did to me?"

As the intolerable heat brought my thoughts back to the present day, I arrived on the block, ignoring jokes from E-Ward and the rest of Rome's workers standing outside of Felipe's Bodega.

Still confused by early childhood memories, I entered Felipe's dimly lit store, hearing the echo of Spanish music throughout the aisles.

After grabbing a bottle of water, I stood behind Poddy Pod, who was arguing with Felipe about the price of matches.

"A Papi, are you for real, ten cents for one book of matches!"

Felipe stood behind the cash register with his skinny arms folded across his chest, while a look of disgust glowed on his tan-colored face.

"Look pa-pa, if you don't like, you go buy somewhere else, okay!"

With his neon colored sunglasses glued to his forehead, Poddy Pod slowly adjusted the rope tied around his thin waist, while pretending to look for loose change in the pockets of his dirty jeans.

"Felipe, you can't look out for me baby?" Poddy Pod asked.

"No pa-pa, not this time, you no do nothing for me or yourself!"

Poddy Pod pulled out some napkins from his pocket, wiping sweat off of his dark colored neck.

"Oh you think you know what it's like to walk in my shoes, uh. Well let me tell something my Dominican friend, just thank GOD that you've never had something control every piece of your life."

Just as I was going to offer to pay for Poddy Pod's matches, we all turned our heads to the screeching sound of tires, followed by a series of rapid gunfire.

While everyone in the store was in the process of dropping to the floor, multiple bullets had already shattered the front door glass of Felipe's.

One of the bullets was so close to my head that I heard it whistling as it passed by my ear.

Attempting to figure out my next move, I quickly grabbed my gun, watching Poddy Pod's blood seal the cracks of Felipe's tiled floor.

Minutes later, the gunshots stopped, as I stood on both feet, clinching a weapon that I wasn't ready use.

For a short moment, I glanced down at Poddy Pod's wounded head, as the puddle of blood next to his thin body, grew larger.

Just as I was making my exit, Felipe started to shout Spanish words through a cordless phone, most likely toward the police or ambulance department.

I immediately ran outside of the store, noticing pieces of brick chipped off the wall from stray bullets, but also realizing there wasn't a soul in sight.

Clueless as to why this happened, I ran through the trash infested alleys, noticing E-Ward leaning against the backdoor of an abandoned house, with blood covering his powder blue shirt.

"E-Wizzy you alright?" I asked.

"Naw man, I've been shot, look you gotta help me get to my wheels!"

"Where's your car at?"

"It's parked near your house."

Praying silently, I helped E-Ward stand up straight, as police sirens yelled from a close distance.

Although we couldn't walk at a normal pace, we still managed to make it to E-Ward's car unnoticed, until a four door Nissan pulled up alongside of us.

The bald headed driver, who was dressed in business attire, immediately exited his vehicle to offer me assist with E-Ward.

"Here, let's lay him across my back seat!" Mr. Gilliam said.

I was surprised that Mr. Gilliam was here and willing to help, but despite that, I knew Mr. Gilliam would do whatever was best. Together Mr. Gilliam and I were able to get E-Ward in the car, placing him in a position that seemed most comfortable.

Everyone's clothing was instantly stained with blood, along with the cream colored upholstery of Mr. Gilliam's car.

"A-yo Fat Tah, I want you to sit back here with me!" E-Ward demanded.

I quickly sat in the back seat of the car, elevating

E-Ward's head with my thigh, as he begun to speak in a whispering tone.

"Fat Tah, you gotta tell Mr. Gilliam to get me to the hospital a little faster than this!"

"We're on our way right now!" I replied.

Driving as if there were sirens on the roof of his car, Mr. Gilliam ignored red lights, reaching speeds up to 65mph on tightly spaced city streets.

Uncertain as to how Mr. Gilliam would respond, I honored E-Ward's request.

"Mr. Gilliam, please step on it!"

"I'm sorry Fat Tah, but I can't go no faster than this!" Mr. Gilliam quickly replied.

The car seemed to be moving slower than the speedometer reported, but sadly E-Ward was losing blood at a much higher speed.

"I'm sorry GOD, I'm really sorry!" E-Ward mumbled.

I wasn't sure as to what E-Ward was sorry about, but I figured that was between him and GOD.

"Fat Tah, do you pray?"

"Yeah, I pray every day!" I answered.

"Do you really think GOD forgives people, no matter what they've done?"

I remained silent, wishing that GOD would never forgive my predator for what he had done to my life.

"Well Fat Tah, I need GOD's forgiveness right now!" E-Ward continued to mumble.

As we got closer to the Hospital, E-Ward's eyes began to flicker like light switches, as blood must have been entering his lungs, muffling every word he spoke.

"I didn't mean to shoot them, but I was nervous and Rome had got me so high, that I would have killed anything that day!"

"E-Wizzy, what in the world are you talking about?" I asked, while embracing his bloody hands.

"I look into their painted eyes every day, wishing they would have never come in the store, but also wishing I was never there too!"

At that moment, I couldn't believe what was just told to me, but oddly I couldn't figure out why E-Ward revealed his secret to me.

Mr. Gilliam quickly parked in front of the compact Emergency Room entrance, determined to save E-Ward from dying.

Feeling a strange increase in E-Ward's body weight, we attempted to lift him out of the discolored back seat, as the hospital staff helped place him on a stretcher.

During this process, E-Ward did not speak a word, nor did his eyes open to observe his surroundings.

Inhaling stale air, as Mr. Gilliam and I followed the team of doctors and nurses into the hospital, we were eventually assigned to a waiting room, until further notice.

While stationed in the waiting area, my thoughts were taken captive by the images of nature and calm sceneries plastered along the walls. Mr. Gilliam sat across the room on a wooden sofa as the bags underneath his eyes expanded with unreleased tears.

"Fat Tah I apologize, I didn't even ask if you got hurt out there, as well."

"Naw, I'm alright Mr. Gilliam, I just want E-Ward to be okay."

"Yeah, I'm praying for the same thing."

Moments later Mr. Gilliam begun to loosen the red necktie resting upon his soiled shirt, as I continued to fantasize about being somewhere as peaceful as the pictures on the wall.

"Hey Fat Tah, I'm sure you know that Murray got locked up."

"Yeah Mr. Gilliam, I heard about that!"

"Well, this time Murray is going to be charged as an adult, because he was the main suspect in a murder connected with the carjacking of a red Cadillac. Also, the police found a gun on him, along with four hundred bags of crack cocaine, inside of this carjacked Cadillac, he was driving."

Mr. Gilliam slowly shook his bald rectangular head, while wiping away tears from his watery eyes.

"Fat Tah, I watched each and every one of you boys and girls from that block, grow from babies to teenagers, and I also watched your boy Rome, grow up as well. Each and every one of you young people that hang on that corner have been blessed with a GOD given talent, but the problem is that each person from that corner has only grown physically, not mentally or spiritually, which means that you all will be lacking the key ingredients for a successful life on this planet."

Feeling as if I had been insulted, I knew inside my heart that Mr. Gilliam was right, but I wasn't willing to verbalize it, so I scrunched my eyebrows together, responding in my defense.

"Mr. Gilliam I don't know what you're talking about, but I'm a grown man!"

"Fat Tah, are you sure?" Mr. Gilliam asked sarcastically.

"More than sure, I make money all day and I don't ask nobody for nothing!"

"Well Fat Tah, being a man involves more than just making money. Being a man involves self control, self discipline, respect for community, respect for self, respect for life, and most of all respect for your creator, no matter what issues occur in your life. You see Fat Tah, the selling drugs is killing the community as a whole, because the drugs devastate the lives of the users, which eventually kills every ounce of dignity and self control they've ever possessed, ultimately destroying that person's family, and I know you've experienced this personally."

"Mr. Gilliam, with all due respect, please don't judge me, because you ain't walked two steps in my shoes."

After I replied, Mr. Gilliam instantly removed a brown

leather wallet from his blazer that contained a picture of what appeared to be an impoverished elderly couple, standing in front of a tin shack.

"This here is a picture of my great grandparents, who lived on a plantation in the South. They instilled values in my family that have never been forgotten, oh did I mention they couldn't read or write, but passed along positive qualities about life, that never embraced hatred, despite the circumstances they had to endure. Although both of my birth parents were killed in a car accident, my grandparents, whose parents were former slaves, emphasized the importance of understanding world history. Through doing so, I've learned that during various periods in history, every nationality of people in the world, have suffered at the hands of other humans with ill intended plans.

Right now, my son Murray, you, and the rest of the younger generation are causing our communities to suffer and sadly these murderous messages and activities are being reinforced daily, if you need proof just turn on your radio or television."

"I hear you Mr. Gilliam, but what do you expect me to do, I'm only one person, but right now I need to go to the bathroom and we'll talk when I get back."

Following my quick departure from the waiting area, I noticed two rigid faced Camden City Police Officers and a doctor walking into the waiting room. Most likely they wanted to question Mr. Gilliam and me, but I decided to exit the crowded hospital before any questions could be directed my way.

CHAPTER

5

F^{requently} looking behind me, I traveled with a sense of urgency, quickly removing my blood-stained T-shirt to avoid any unwanted attention.

Although the sun's heat would be rough on the bare skin of my chubby frame, I continued my escape feeling sweat rollercoaster off of my body.

"Oils, T-shirts, Water!" A short pop-bellied man yelled from across the street.

At that moment I thanked GOD, quickly crossing the congested street, as the small weapon lay hidden in my underwear.

"Hey my shirtless brotha, what you need is one of these T-shirts and a bottle of water!" the pop-bellied man offered.

Nodding my head with agreement, I removed some money from my pocket and purchased a T-shirt, foolishly refusing the water.

Shortly after traveling a few city blocks, I escaped to the rear of a local business and re-adjusted the small weapon inside of my pants. While doing so, my unspoken emotions pleaded for freedom, but remained controlled by the life sentence of tragedy.

Quickly returning back to my mission, I soon arrived at the public transportation center, ignoring painful thoughts of walking on foot to my part of town.

While awaiting my bus, the summer atmosphere displayed no mercy on the sweat drenched faces surrounding me, which made me wonder if GOD's mercy would be as tough on E-Ward.

Then suddenly I was greeted by warm air and the smell of corn chips, as the doors to my bus opened.

Exercising hurried movements, I stepped onto the crowded bus, instantly attacked by piercing stares from unfamiliar faces. Although I wasn't initially concerned about the tightly packed atmosphere, I began to feel annoyed, while clinching onto my last ounce of sanity.

"Hey young fella, you can sit here if you want," a gray haired man offered, as he wrote inside of a notebook.

Feeling honored amongst the weary occupants standing in the aisle, I immediately sat down, wiping small beads of sweat from my forehead.

"Yeah young brotha, I could tell you've had a long d y and it's probably gonna get a lot longer, trust me!"

Overwhelmed with curiosity, I extended my hand a d introduced myself, internally seeking words of comfo.t from this gray haired stranger.

"Pleasure to meet you Fat Tah, but this is my stop, so I guess I'll see you around."

As the man stood up, his wrinkled fingers ripped a blank piece of paper from his notebook, politely placing it upon my lap.

"Mister, what do I do with this?" I quickly asked.

"Nothing, just let the pain in your heart tell your story, instead of always being a character in someone else's!"

Attempting to unscramble this message, my eyes gazed deeper into the blank paper, opening mental closets of locked memories.

Minutes later, the bus arrived at my stop, unloading a small crowd of fatigued passengers, as I exited with scattered thoughts resting on my fingertips.

"Yo Fat Tah, come here!" A familiar voice yelled from nearby.

Turning my head, I realized it was Dre, sitting on the steps of a local rooming house, which Rome would use for business when the street corners were flooded with police.

Remembering yesterday's episode with Dre, I cautiously approached the steps, as the aroma of weed smoke cluttered the air.

"Whatz up Dre?"

"Yo, E-Ward got to be dead, cuz he got hit up wit like twenty shots; all in the chest I heard!"

"What!" I shouted, while noticing empty bags of weed and cocaine, resting next to Dre's stainless sneakers.

Speaking through chapped lips, badly in need of Vaseline, Dre continued his foolishness.

"Well it don't matta anyway, I don't really care if that dude is dead or paralyzed, I'm gonna be running the block, so now- you- work- under- Dre, you feel me!"

Angered by Dre's arrogance, my suspicions rose as to who and why E-Ward was killed, but to my surprise I maintained my cool, leaving Dre's presence in a speechless fashion.

Amazed by my level of self-control, I rewarded myself with a cigarette as I begun to walk home. Laughing to myself, I remembered my short conversation with Mr. Gilliam, as he said "self-control" was part of being a man.

During this short journey to my house, I saw nobody on the street corners, as several unmarked police cars flooded the area. This was a common practice, whenever somebody got shot, so I knew walking to my house was going to be more difficult, than expected.

Then like an angel dropped from the sky, I saw Talianna and her baby walking toward my direction.

"Hey Fat Tah," Talianna said, in a saddened tone.

As I greeted her with a comforting hug, her skinny arms embraced my body, while cold tear drops penetrated my shirt.

"Whatz goin on family, why you soundin like dat?" I asked, although I knew part of the reason for her pain.

"I've been walking the streets for hours, looking for somebody who is gone forever, and to tell you the truth, I'm tired Fat Tah. I'm tired of all the killings and everybody thinking it's cool, the drug dealing, and everybody thinking that it's alright and not bothering nobody. But most of all Fat Tah, I'm tired of me, because I've always thought those things were "okay," until my son lost his father last night, so in reality those things ain't okay and never were!" she said, as her freshly manicured hands wiped away fallen tears.

Surprised by Talianna's mature view on life, I began wondering if Mr. Gilliam had told her the same things he said to me.

"Talianna, where you and da little one about to go?"

"We was about to go to Felipe's and get something to eat, but it's police tape out dere cause Poddy-Pod and E-Ward got killed."

Curious as to how she was so sure E-Ward died, I asked. "How you know E-Ward died?"

"C'mon Fat Tah, dis is da hood and it don't take long for any news to travel anywhere at any given time, plus I heard two of the cops talking about it, as I tried to get to Felipe's." she said, while adjusting the arm bracelets resting on her cocoa buttered skin.

"Well look family, I gotta go make a move, so you take care of yourself and I promise I'll stop by your house later, to check on you and da baby."

Slowly wrapping her arms around my chubby body, Talianna's soft voice whispered in my ear, "Be safe Fat Tah."

I nodded my head with agreement as our bodies separated, knowing in my heart that change was needed, but I wasn't sure when it was coming.

As Talianna walked in the opposite direction, I paused for a moment and started to adore the gracefulness of her every movement, fantasizing about her soft lips whispering "I love you Fat Tah."

Quickly interrupted by the distant sound of police sirens, I returned from my romantic interlude greeted by the sight of a buggy eyed woman, riding alongside some elderly man in a white truck.

Shortly after driving past me, the truck stopped at the corner, as I recognized the woman as my mom, who was exiting the passenger side of the vehicle.

After exiting the truck, she quickly adjusted her tight fitting skirt and placed an unknown amount of money into her bra.

As the truck drove away, my mother began walking toward my direction, but on the opposite side of the street. She was walking so fast, that she never saw me, as her skinny frame disappeared into the hallways of Rome's rooming house.

Saddened by this picture, I felt like killing each and every person that ever sold drugs, as my reflection remained trapped in the windows of a passing car, which made me wonder how many people wanted to kill me.

"That's two fat boy!"

"What!" I said, realizing a Camden City Police car was directly in front of me.

"Listen, this is the second time I drove past here and seen you standing in that same spot!" The officer shouted, while delivering a piercing stare.

"Sorry about that officer, I was just arguing with my girl, so I was just standing here thinking of a way to tell her I'm sorry, you feel me."

"Whatever man, just don't let me see you again, because if I do, you're gonna have a problem!" The officer said, as he turned on his overhead lights and sped away.

Happy that the officer had to leave, I quickly walked to my house, noticing the strange sight of Dre and Big Ede riding in a car with oversized rims. Ignoring the urge to play detective, I entered my house, with memories of Rodney, E-Ward, and Murray running through my mind.

After removing my dirty clothes and stashing Rome's money, I placed the small handgun underneath my pillow, with fearful thoughts of being the next person to die.

While in the shower, I prayed that the slow dripping water would wash away today's experiences, realizing that death was final with no chances of a return, but also that I needed to slow down before I ended up dead or in jail like Murray.

"There's more to being a man than just making money!" replayed in my head, as I exited the shower and returned to my room.

While in my cluttered room, I searched for clothes to wear, hearing the front door of my house close shut, causing me to reach underneath my pillow, for a weapon that was no longer there.

"Unbelievable!" I shouted out loud, while quickly getting dressed and grabbing Rome's money from the small hole in my bedroom ceiling.

After counting at least two thousand dollars, I ran out of my house, with hopes of catching up to my mom, knowing that she wasn't going very far to sell the gun.

As I sprinted down my city block, I was quickly tackled and handcuffed by undercover cops, exiting three different vehicles.

"Yeah, we got him!" a tall muscular cop shouted through

a police radio.

"Got me for what?" I asked, thinking of the many things I've done wrong in the past.

"C'mon fat-boy, let me guess, you just got your income tax check!" A scruffy bearded officer joked, while removing Rome's money from my pockets.

"Where's the drugs at?" The tall muscular cop asked, while searching the area where I was running.

As the undercover cops searched the area for drugs, that same gray Ford, I warned Dre about, parked alongside the other cars, with someone shouting out of the passenger side window, "That's not the guy who ran on us, he's too fat!"

At that moment, I exhaled a sigh of relief, as the undercover cops removed the handcuffs and returned Rome's money back to me.

Clueless as to where my mom was at, I walked toward Talianna's house, as she sat on the steps, while talking through a cordless phone.

"You want me to come back later," I said, while staring into her hazel eyes.

"No Fat Tah, I'm just talking to my brother Cuk!" Talianna said, while pulling on my hand to sit down next to her.

"Why is dat meatball at the house?" Cuk shouted through the phone.

"Once again Cuk, mind your business and stop trying to be in mine, plus you and ya boy Rome are together, doing only GOD knows what," she said, before hanging up the phone.

Then seconds after ending her conversation with Cuk, sounds of a baby crying exited from her house.

"Don't leave Fat Tah, I just have to give the baby his bottle," Talianna said, as she sprinted into the house, leaving behind a pleasant scent.

While awaiting Talianna's return, I saw Dre and Big Ede once again, driving that same car with the oversized rims.

"Yoooo Fat Tah!" Big Ede yelled out of the driver side window, while bringing the car to a stop.

I didn't reply to Big Ede, knowing that he tried to rob me the other night, but I knew something was about happen because he and Dre both exited the car and were now walking toward me with devilish smiles and blood stained eyes.

CHAPTER

6

"Well Fat Tah, where's dat money you was supposed to give me?" Big Ede asked, while swinging car keys around his massive fingertips.

"Ohhh, that money!" I sarcastically said, before darting down the street.

Big Ede and Dre chased me for about one block, until I leaped over a small silver fence landing into a yard full of angry pit-bulls.

"Yeah, I got you now fat-boy!" Big Ede said as I quickly climbed out of the yard of blood thirsty dogs.

Dre and Big Ede attacked me with a flurry of bone crushing punches, as the pit-bulls barked uncontrollably from behind the small fence.

Big Ede was able to remove some of the money from my pockets, but couldn't get it all, as I delivered three punches to his bumpy face.

"Give up da money Fat Tah!" Dre yelled, as he started to kick my bloodied face, allowing Big Ede to remove the rest of the money from my pockets.

Unable to speak a word, my eyes widened to the sight of Big Ede and Dre removing guns from their waist area. Although I couldn't see very clearly, I noticed that the gun Dre was holding in his hand looked just like the gun Rome had given me.

"Hey, who's that in back of my house?" The voice of an elderly woman yelled.

Realizing that witnesses were around, Dre and Big Ede ran away, leaving my beaten body hurt to the core, but still alive.

While lying with my back on the ground, I could smell the strong odor of dog waste as the sun disappeared behind moon.

"Hey boy, are you alright?" an elderly woman asked, while exiting her back door.

"Yeah I'm okay!"

"Well, let me help you up!" the woman said, while walking through her yard of pit-bulls.

As the woman opened her gate, three dark colored pit-bulls walked alongside of her, as she helped me stand up.

"Put your arm around my shoulders and walk with me!" the elderly woman said, while adjusting her red housecoat.

As we entered her house, the aroma of fried chicken filled the air, as she guided my beaten body to a small bathroom next to her kitchen.

"So young-man, why were those guys beating on you like that?" the elderly woman asked, as she began to apply peroxide to my wounds.

"I don't know, they just wanted to rob me, I guess."

"Yeah, the same way you and those boys at that corner store have been robbing this community for years!"

"Huhhh!" I said, as the muscular shaped dogs watched

my every movement, from outside of the tiny bathroom.

"Oh yeah, I know who you are, I've seen you down at the corner for years, I also seen when you jumped out of my yard and into the hands of those boys, who did this to you!"

"Look lady, I appreciate your help, but I'm not about to be lectured about what I do!"

After nursing my wounds, the elderly lady exited the bathroom and began feeding her hungry dogs pieces of fried chicken.

"Are you hungry young man?"

"To be real wit you Miss, I am hungry!" I said, while embracing no memories of having a home cooked meal, since my grandmother died.

"Well I am happy to see that you're not shy, I hope you like fried chicken and biscuits, because that's what's on the menu for tonight," she said, while delivering a smile, as warm as the food she served.

While eating one of the best meals, I had eaten in years I could feel the smooth fur of the dogs rubbing against my legs.

"Looks like my little ones have found a new friend," the lady said, while placing buttered biscuits on my plate.

Just as the biscuits dropped softly to my plate, sounds of rapid gunfire echoed from a distance, for almost five minutes long.

Angered and disturbed by the unpleasant sound of gunfire, the elderly woman shook her gray colored head from side to side, while wiping away tears with the sleeves of her housecoat.

"Young man, God has blessed me with seventy-one years on this earth and I've lived here at this house all of my life. I choose to stay here because this is my community and I care about this community. I just want you younger folk to start caring it about too, especially before nobody is left that cares about it, or even wants to care about it. Young man, I don't know you personally, but I do know that those fellas, who beat you up were going to kill you, so basically GOD saved your life!"

Turning my head away from the elderly woman, I looked at the walls of her house, seeing pictures of Dr. Martin Luther King Jr., President JFK, future President Barack Obama, and many other black and white faces of worldly influence. This house seemed like a history museum, as newspaper clippings from the 70's and 60's were framed or wrapped in plastic.

"Respect the community surrounding you and you will learn a lot!" she said, while directing the dogs out into the backyard.

"Why do you collect all this stuff?" I asked while walking toward her plastic covered couches.

"My children are adults now, but when they were children, I felt that it was important for them to learn as much as possible. So I took the responsibility of teaching them different skills, so that they could avoid learning the things that led to nothing but jail terms and graves!"

"I wish I had somebody to teach me these things," I said, not realizing that I was thinking out loud.

"You have Mrs. Lacey to do that for you," the elderly woman said.

"Who's Mrs. Lacey?" I asked.

"That me, silly!"

"Ohhh, well my name is Fat Tah." I said, not understanding why she would be willing to help me, especially knowing that I sell drugs not even a full block away from her home.

"Listen Fat Tah, life is about choices and you can choose to be a drug dealer or murderer, or you can choose to do things to help the world like future President Barack Obama, President JFK, and Dr. Martin Luther King Jr., or you can make a lasting imprint on your community, like Murray Gilliam, the block captain. Mr. Fat Tah, I am dedicated to helping you and whomever else wants help, but I can only help you if you are willing to remain focused and give up the negative things in life, so that your future is positive."

"I'll keep that in mind Mrs. Lacey!" I said while slowly limping toward the front door.

"I know you will Fat Tah, and by the way you can stop by here anytime you want, maybe I'll show you how to train dogs, so that they don't eat you up next time you're getting chased." she smilingly said.

While exiting Mrs. Lacey's house I remembered that I needed to go back to Talianna's, to at least let her know that I didn't leave on purpose, but most of all I needed to find Rome.

When I arrived at Talianna's house, after limping from a block away, she answered the door, while embracing her sleeping child.

"Come in Fat Tah," she whispered, as her long hair rested on the back of an oversized football jersey.

"Sorry about earlier, but I didn't want any craziness to happen in front of your house, especially wit the baby being in here."

"Why is there blood on your shirt Fat Tah, and what are you talking about?" she asked, as I limped further into the air conditioned house.

"While I was waiting for you to finish feeding the baby, some knuckleheads decided to rob me!"

"Ohh my God, I'm sorry Fat Tah, I didn't know!" she screamed, as we both sat down on her mom's leather couch.

"It's cool, I know who did it!"

"Fat Tah, please promise me that you're not planning to get revenge on whoever robbed you?" Talianna begged, as her hazel eyes widened with concern.

"Listen, I just wanted to stop by to let you know that I really was looking forward to spending time with you earlier, but right now I gotta go, because I have to explain what happened to Rome's money."

"No, please don't go Fat Tah, it's not worth it!" she cried out, while positioning the baby on the couch.

Attempting to avoid eye contact with Talianna, I directed my attention toward a large fish tank, located across the carpeted room. While looking into this fish tank, I saw one lonely fish with orange stripes, swimming with no real sense of freedom.

"If I just let dem dudes get away wit robbing me, people from all over this neighborhood is gonna think I'm some type of punk, and I ain't no punk and never will be!"

"Naw you ain't no punk, but you will be stupid, especially if you die over some money, that probably didn't even belong to you or better yet, spend life in jail for murder, like my dad!" She said, while moving her slender body closer to mine.

Exhaling with confusion, I shook my head from side to side, while watching the lonely fish remain trapped by the walls of the tank.

"I don't know what to do!"

"Just believe in yourself, believe that you have the power to control your anger, no matter how mad you get," she whispered softly, while leaning her sweet scented body into my arms.

As I slowly caressed Talianna's smooth skin, every angry thought I possessed, instantly exited my body.

"Fat Tah, do you have somebody you trust?"

"Nobody, except for myself, if that counts," I said, while looking at a graduation picture of Talianna's mom, hanging on the wall.

"For many years of my life I didn't trust anybody and I hated anybody who tried to find out anything about me, and I'll tell you Fat Tah, it hurt like hell, to not have anybody to really open my heart to!"

"Yeah, I know dat feeling, and it does hurt like hell," I said, as years of abuse replayed in my head.

"Fat Tah, when I was a little girl my mom had a boyfriend who lived with us, after my dad got sentenced to life in prison. Now, this boyfriend she had was a very nice guy in the beginning, although he didn't work or pay any bills, but what he did do was get high off of drugs, which led to him saying real freaky and nasty words to me, on a daily basis."

Silenced momentarily by painful memories, Talianna closed her eyes, as I wiped away tears racing down her pudgy cheeks.

"Well, his freaky words eventually led to him raping me almost every day, for a whole year, especially while my mom was at work. I held onto that secret for years, slowly destroying my sanity and most of all, my trust for people. Then one day, long after my mom stopped dating the man, the memories became so bad that I had to leave class and go to the school nurse, because I couldn't stop crying. When I told the nurse what happened, they called my mom and the police, which led to her ex-boyfriend getting locked up.

"So how do you deal with the memories now, since all that happened?" I asked, secretly seeking help with my unspoken memories.

"I have a therapist that I talk to a couple times a month. She's understands my situation, but most of all she helps me to realize that it wasn't my fault. She's teaching me how to deal with my problems, without always looking for an easy way out. Listen Fat Tah, I've had a lot of hurt in my life, especially dealing with the murder of my baby's dad, being raped, and not having my dad around to guide me, but also dealing with the fact that I am a teenage mom. Fat Tah, I feel like I'm a train and every life experience that comes my way is the coal, that burns inside my train to push me further, believe me Fat Tah, I'm no longer afraid to talk about the things that bother me, at least that way I can get solutions and keep anger from destroying me.

CHAPTER

7

"Wow, it must feel good to have people, who care about you!" I said, as my chubby head lowered with sadness.

"Fat Tah we've been friends for a long time, and I know your situation at home is killing you on the inside, but Fat Tah you gotta let it out, especially before you do something that will take you away from me forever."

"You should be a mind reader!" I said, as my heartbeats increased with nervousness.

"I'm here for you Fat Tah, whenever you need me!"

"I know dat family, but sometimes life will deal you a hand that is impossible to play. Sometimes life leaves you with no choices but one, especially when you're a lil' fat kid with a drug addicted mom and a absent dad who was only around long enough to beat up his own son and force him to...!"

At that moment we heard some people arguing outside of Talianna's front door, which was quickly followed by a series of multiple gunshots. As soon as the gun battle started, I grabbed Talianna and threw her to the carpeted floor, while crawling toward the other end of the couch, to get the baby.

"Stay down!" I yelled, as bullets shattered the front window of the house.

Crying and scared, Talianna tightly embraced her startled baby, as the short gun battle came to an end.

Minutes after the gunshots deceased, police cars flooded the area, as a chubby woman wearing a public transportation uniform, entered Talianna's house.

"Baby-girl you alright?" The woman asked, as Talianna cuddled her baby while sitting on the floor.

"Yes mom, we're okay, I was just sitting on the floor because somebody was shooting outside again, and this time they shot out the front window by the couch."

"Thank GOD, you're alright baby, I'm not worried about that window, I'm just worried about my family!" she said, as I stood to my feet.

"How are you doing Ms. Jenkins?"

"I'll be much better once you leave my house young man, it's nothing personal, but drug dealers are not welcomed in my home, just ask your boy Cuk!" Ms. Jenkins said, while attempting to pick up the pieces of glass scattered throughout the carpeted floor.

Realizing Ms. Jenkins was only trying to protect her family I honored her request and exited the house, without speaking a word.

Worried with concern for my life, I slowly limped through alleys blanketed by darkness, as the glowing eyes of stray animals crossed my path.

"I can't believe it, Dre and Big Ede really tried to kill me!" I thought to myself, while entering my house.

During that night, I tried to mentally prepare for Rodney's funeral, wondering if I could have done something to prevent his death.

Shortly afterwards, I fell asleep, only to be awakened by pounding knocks at my front door.

"Who is it?" I asked, as I opened the door.

It was Dre, smiling with red eyes, while pointing a large sized gun in my face.

"Say hello to ya boy Rodney, for me!" he said, while squeezing the trigger.

Jumping out of my bed, drenched with sweat, I realized that it was all a dream, as sunshine filled every corner of my cluttered room.

"I'm really going crazy!" I thought to myself, as I walked toward the bathroom.

After taking a shower and dressing in black jeans and shirt, I walked out of my house toward Felipe's, to meet with everybody from my block, who was going to Rodney's funeral.

When I arrived at Felipe's there was a large crowd standing around drinking and smoking, as some people wore white T-shirts with pictures of Rodney airbrushed on the front and back, while others with the words "In Memory of Rodney" painted on the rear windows of their cars.

While standing amongst the saddened crowd, I saw Cuk exit a black colored SUV, spray painted with white lettering "RIP Rome."

Feeling as if, my older brother just died, I pushed through the smoke filled crowd, until I reached Cuk.

"What happened?" I asked, as my eyes swelled with water pressure.

"Last night, Rome was at a pay phone, a couple of blocks away from here and got into a shootout with some dudes," Cuk said, as his wide hands removed a bottle of liquor from the SUV.

"So he died right there?" I asked, remembering that Talianna said Cuk and Rome were together last night, "doing only GOD knows what."

"No Mr. Investigator, he died in front of his mom's crib, while trying to open the front door, it's a damn shame, cuz if I was there, Rome would be standing with us right now, for real!"

Smelling the strong odor of betrayal, I walked off quietly, while Cuk drank liquor and socialized with the older street veterans from our block.

As I distanced myself from the crowded corner, a dark colored Dodge wagon drove alongside me, slowly lowering its tinted windows.

Instantly, I thought it was Big Ede and Dre, but to my surprise, it turned out to be Mr. Gilliam.

"Fat Tah, you look as if you seen a ghost," Mr. Gilliam said, as the car stopped.

"Yeah I thought I did, Mr. Gilliam, but anyway what you doin driving this car?"

"Well, the other car needs to be detailed because of all the blood stains on the upholstery, so I rented this car so that I could still get to work, but right now I'm on my way to the funeral home and I wanted to know if you would ride with me."

"Yeah, I'll ride with you," I quickly responded, as Mr. Gilliam relocated some religious literature to the back seat of the car.

When I entered the car, Mr. Gilliam and I shook hands, as wordless music exited the speakers.

"Mr. Gilliam, what in the world are you listening too?" I asked, while hearing different musical instruments harmonize together.

"It's called jazz, Fat Tah, this kind of music allows my thoughts to be at ease, instead of being upset or frustrated all the time."

"Kinda like music for your soul," I said, with a smile on my chubby face.

"Yes sir, it most definitely is."

As we began our journey to the funeral home, Mr. Gilliam purposely drove at a slow pace, while pointing his thin fingers toward vacant lots and parks full of trash.

Most of the areas we drove through were flooded with drug dealing teenagers, who delivered unfriendly stares, while standing in front of graffiti stained walls and rows of abandoned houses.

"Fat Tah, could you do me a favor and count all the "RIP" memorials you see as we drive to the funeral home?" Mr. Gilliam asked, while continuing to drive slowly.

"Mr. Gilliam, it's too many to count, man I can think of five people that have been killed in the past two weeks, and that's just from my block!"

"How many of those people were over the age of twenty, or even completed high school, Fat Tah?"

"Maybe one out of the five, but listen Mr. Gilliam that don't have nothing to do with me."

Providing no response, Mr. Gilliam adjusted his necktie as he changed the radio station to music, which glorified the lifestyles of drug dealers and murders.

Moments later, we arrived at the crowded funeral home, seeing people of all ages, as well as uniformed police officers standing outside.

"Why is it so many cops out here?" I asked, while exiting the car.

"I guess since Rodney was murdered the other day and Rome was murdered last night, the police are probably trying to prevent anyone else from getting killed," Mr. Gilliam explained, as he activated the alarm to his rental car.

When we entered the dimly lit funeral home full of teary eyed people, Mr. Gilliam immediately sat with Rodney's sobbing mom, Ms. Douglas, as I patiently waited in line to have a final talk with my best friend.

As I arrived at the flower draped casket, I looked at Rodney's sleeping body, realizing his folded hands, no longer had to pass out bags of crack, or fight with peers over childish arguments, but also his closed eyes would never have to open to the harsh realities of living in a war zone.

"What up Rod?" I softly whispered. "I know you safe, so whatever you're doin I know you don't have to worry bout being locked up, or wishing you could see the world, cuz GOD is gonna let you live out your dreams in the comfort of his arms. I'm tryin to be a better person, with the help of some good people, but it's so hard because I got so much on my plate, but I'm gonna keep tryin, you feel me. Listen out for my prayers, while you up there, and ask GOD to shower the world with his blessing, cuz it's too crazy right now. Well look I gotta go, but remember Rod, I luv you and don't be gettin into no trouble wit Rome, cuz he'll get you kicked out of heaven for sure. Peace!"

While slowly walking away from the casket, my watery eyes located an empty spot along the wood-paneled wall, figuring that this was the best spot to be at, since there were no seats available amongst the mourning crowd.

Then as the line leading to Rodney's casket disappeared, Mr. Gilliam walked to the front of the room, staring silently at the crowd as he removed his dark colored suit jacket and necktie.

"First off I want to thank Ms. Douglas for allowing me to say a few words. I'm not here today to just talk about the loss of this young man, but what I am here to talk about, is the fact that senseless violence has become acceptable, drug dealing has become acceptable, disrespect for females has become acceptable, and the trading of our souls for material objects has become acceptable. I don't understand this philosophy, but it seems the more I try to understand it, the more hurt I experience. Yesterday I found out that my son will probably spend the next thirty years in prison, as a result of poor decision making. Poor decision making and the acceptance of peer pressure have contributed to his actions, as well as to the actions of many of the other youth in our city. Poor decision making has led to the murder of this young man laying in this casket, because I'm willing to bet that whoever killed him was probably under the influence of drugs, peer pressure or didn't realize that the amount of money and drugs they took from him didn't amount to the loss of precious years that they'll spend in jail, once caught by the police!"

Following that statement, some of Rodney's family members began to mumble comments of disapproval, as Mr. Gilliam remained firm and unmoved by their words.

"Look people I'm not gonna sit up here and sugar coat anything, or make somebody seem like a saint, when they weren't. Now if I can talk about my son, I'll definitely tell the truth about someone else's child. Rodney wasn't a bad child, but he was misled and made poor decisions.

We as a community have to start being responsible for our own children and property, as well as the children and property of others in our neighborhood. That doesn't mean that some people won't gravitate toward negative things; look at my son for example, but what it does mean is that if I see people loitering in front my neighbor's house, selling drugs I'm calling the police about it, but before I do that I'll go speak to the group and let them know what I'm doing. We can no longer be afraid to approach the people who are tearing down our neighborhoods, because that's how our neighborhoods have gotten to the poor condition there in right now. Some people in this room have been incarcerated at one point in their lives, but have probably not told the youth or their friends about the bad days in jail, when they were crying or attacked by others. Our youth don't need to hear any glory stories about being locked up or committing crimes, because it's making them believe that they'll have a better opportunity of going to jail, before achieving a high school diploma or attending college. As a community we have to establish some programs that will allow these youth to practice their talents and most of all learn about business, since so many of them end up selling drugs." Mr. Gilliam smilingly said.

"We must show these young men and women about the proper way to generate money, not through methods that will surely result in death or imprisonment. This is a serious topic, but it can only begin to work with the cooperation of both the young and the old.

While continuing his lengthy speech, Mr. Gilliam used a cream colored handkerchief to remove sweat from his rectangular head.

Finally, I want the youth to begin to think about their mind and bodies as cars. I say cars because cars need gasoline to run, and periodically they need check-ups. Which means you can't put soda in your gas tank and expect the car to work properly, because it is not gonna happen. Your bodies need to be drug and alcohol free so that your brains can work properly and that you all can make choices that will ultimately benefit your lives, not destroy them. Young people you also need to associate yourselves with positive people, so that when you are making mistakes, they can be the one's who'll try to get you back on the right path. Also my young people, be careful of the types of television shows you watch and the type of music you listen too, as well as the type of people you surround yourselves with, on a daily basis. I believe that if you listen to people, music, and watch shows about constant murdering and drug selling, you'll begin to view it as being acceptable, but in reality those things are not acceptable and only lead to jail and graves. I thank you for listening, but I strongly urge you all to begin transforming your lives for the benefit of your community, as the next doctor, scientist, nurse, president, school teacher, community leader, store owner or daycare provider is sitting or standing next to you will probably be killed before they have the opportunity to decide on their future."

Following that last statement, Mr. Gilliam turned and whispered some final goodbyes to Rodney, before leaving behind a quiet audience of thinkers, as he exited the funeral home.

Realizing Mr. Gilliam was probably the most influential person in my life I shoved and pushed through the tightly packed aisle, to catch up with him, before he attempted to drive away in his car.

"Mr. Gilliam, I really liked the speech you just gave and I'm honestly ready to change my life, for the benefit of my future, plus as a man I must be disciplined to achieve my goals!" I shouted at the top of my lungs, as Mr. Gilliam attempted to open his car door.

Staring with a smile as wide as the ocean, Mr. Gilliam walked toward me, tightly wrapping his skinny arms around my chubby body.

"I'm so proud of you Fat Tah, I really am!" Mr. Gillam yelled, as he delivered the warmest and most sincere hug I've ever felt.

During the months that followed, I entered my senior year of high school and was now working for a local fast food restaurant on the weekends, while also making money by walking Mrs. Lacey's dogs, for her. Some nights I would go to Mrs. Lacey's house with Talianna and Mrs. Lacey would teach us how to cook different foods as well as teach us about historical events that have led to the growth of our nation as a whole.

Surprisingly, Mr. Gilliam became the father that I never had, and I guess I became his second son, as we spent countless hour's together working on community projects such as litter patrol and teen literacy, along with the help of Talianna.

Murray, who was now serving thirty-five years in Federal Prison, frequently sent letters of praise to Mr. Gilliam, thanking him for being an excellent father, but also apologizing for his own criminal behavior.

Big Ede and Dre never did end up taking control of the block. They were arrested two weeks after Rodney's funeral for the murders of E-Ward, Poddy-Pod, and Rodney as well. In addition, they faced charges for three different homicides and both were sentenced to life in prison.

As for Cuk, he gained control of the block for about one month, but was eventually arrested and sentenced to seventeen years in prison, for the murder of Rome.

Things down at Felipe's remained the same, but just with new faces who felt they wouldn't make the same mistakes that got the previous group of people arrested.

As for my unspoken memories, Mr. Gilliam was introduced me to a therapist that really gained my trust and was able to assist me in coping with my childhood memories of sexual and physical abuse. I couldn't believe that I was able to discuss those horrific memories, without being judged or laughed at.

I honestly feel that my therapist had a true understanding of who I am, but mainly I no longer allow those hurtful memories to steal my joy, although I'm not saying I don't have bad days, but now I have the tools and confidence to change the bad feelings to positive qualities.

Striving to experience the power of growth, I remained focused and determined to change my life, as I completed my final year of high school, without any further criminal involvement.

Two weeks after I graduated from high school, my mother enrolled in a drug and alcohol program, to address her addiction issues. Now she attends treatment several times a week and our relationship has improved greatly, especially since I informed her and the rest of the people inside of my circle of positive friends about my acceptance into community college.

I am now driving my life in a direction that'll keep

me from prison or committing crimes, but most of all I mentor youth reminding them that we all get knocked down in the fight to save our lives, but we must get up and sometimes we have to ask for help to win that fight, just look at my experience with growth.

DISCUSSION

QUESTIONS

1. What steps must I take, in order to make all of my
   dreams a reality?

   _____

   _____

   _____

   _____

   _____

   _____

2. What are my plans for the next few years?

   _____

   _____

   _____

   _____

   _____

3. Does my anger often lead to negative situations?

   _____

   _____

   _____

   _____

   _____

4. Who are the most positive people in my life?

   _____

   _____

   _____

   _____

   _____

5. Who are the most negative people in my life?

_____
_____
_____
_____
_____
_____

6. Who is willing to help me change my life?

_____
_____
_____
_____
_____
_____

7. What role does education play in my future plans?

_____
_____
_____
_____
_____
_____

8. How often do I give into peer pressure?

_____
_____
_____
_____
_____
_____

9. What are the benefits to living a drug and alcohol free lifestyle?

_____
_____

The Experience of Growth

CONTACT INFORMATION

To schedule speaking appearances or to order copies of the book, contact Robert Bayard at robbayard77@ yahoo.com.

Resources

Sexual & Physical Abuse

www.counselingcorner.net
www.centerforhealing.net
www.crosscreekcounseling.com/sexual_abuse.html
www.delosuicideprevention.org
www.centerffs.org
www.nhsonline.org

Youth Mentoring Programs

www.volunteersolutions.org
www.youthmentoring.org
www.solutionsforamerica.org
www.friendsforyouth.org
www.ytc.net

Youth Programs

www.bgcphila.org
www.bandgccc.org
www.bgcnj.org
www.hopeworks.org

This list of programs may help individuals and their families locate assistance, when needed

NOTES

NOTES

NOTES

NOTES

NOTES

NOTES

NOTES

NOTES

NOTES

CPSIA information can be obtained
at www.ICGtesting.com
Printed in the USA
FFOW04n0656250615
14523FF